MR. MEN and LITTLE MISS™ © THOIP (a Chorion Company)

www.mrmen.com

Mr. Men and Little Miss™ Text and illustrations
© 2010 THOIP (a Chorion company).
Printed and published under licence from
Price Stern Sloan, Inc., Los Angeles.

Original creation by Roger Hargreaves
Illustrated by Adam Hargreaves
First published in Great Britain 1998
This edition published in Great Britain in 2010 by Dean,
an imprint of Egmont UK Limited
239 Kensington High Street, London W8 6SA

Printed in Italy
ISBN 978 0 6035 6568 7

1 3 5 7 9 10 8 6 4 2

LITTLE MISS HELPFUL

AND THE
GREEN HOUSE

Roger Hargreaves

DEAN

With a name like Helpful you would think that Little Miss Helpful would be helpful, wouldn't you?

Well, you'd be wrong.

She wanted to help people more
than anything else in the world,
but as hard as she tried she always
ended up being unhelpful.

One day, about a week ago, Little Miss Helpful was sitting on a bus on her way to town.

Mr Slow and Mr Happy were sitting in front of her having a conversation.

"I ... wish ... I ... had ... a ... green ... house ... but ... I ... never ... get ... the ... time ... to ... do ... anything," said Mr Slow to Mr Happy.

It was a very slow conversation.

Just then the bus stopped.

Now, what Little Miss Helpful had just overheard had given her an idea.

She got off the bus.

And walked across to Mr Nail's Hardware store, and bought all the green paint that he had.

Then Mr Nail delivered all the green
paint to ... Mr Slow's house.

I am sure you can guess what she had
in mind.

That's right.

She was going to surprise Mr Slow by helping him paint his house green.

Helpful Little Miss Helpful!

Little Miss Helpful started to paint.

She painted all the walls.

She painted all the doors.

She painted the chimney and
the roof!

She even painted all the windows.

The window panes as well as
the frames!

When she had finished painting
the house she still had some paint
left over.

So she painted the garage as well.

Outside and inside!

Little Miss Helpful was terribly
pleased with herself.

She stood back to admire
her handiwork.

It was then that Mr Slow arrived
back home.

In the time it had taken Miss Helpful
to paint his house he had bought a
loaf of bread.

He isn't called Mr Slow for nothing.

Mr Slow had to look twice before he realised that his house was still there.

"What ... have ... you ... done?"
he exclaimed.

"You said that you wanted a green
house," said Miss Helpful, "so there
you are."

"That's ... not ... what ... I ... meant. I ... want ... a ... greenhouse," said Mr Slow.

"Exactly," said Miss Helpful. "And I painted your house green."

"No I ... want ... the ... sort ... of ... greenhouse ... that ... you ... grow ... tomatoes ... in," explained Mr Slow, slowly.

"Oh ..." said Little Miss Helpful.

" ... then what colour did you want your house to be?"

Mr Slow groaned a very slow groan.
He could see it was going to be a
very long afternoon.

Even for him!